I Can't Open It

Paul Shipton

Illustrated by Claire Chrystall

Chelsea and Harry went
to the book shop.

BOOKSHOP

Pull

Book
Sale
Book
Sale

Harry pushed and pushed.
"I can't open this door,"
he said.

"Don't push," said Chelsea.
"Pull."
Harry pulled.
The door opened.

Then Chelsea and Harry
went to the toy shop.

TOY SHOP

Push

9

Harry pulled and pulled.
"I can't open this door,"
he said.

"Don't pull," said Chelsea.
"Push."
Harry pushed.
The door opened.

Then Chelsea and Harry
went to the supermarket.

SUPERMARKET

Automatic

½ Price

15